# TRANSFORM YOUR
# MSME2
# MNC

**Let's Begin Your Journey To BuildMNC**

# TRANSFORM YOUR MSME2 MNC

**Let's Begin Your Journey To BuildMNC**

## CMA. PANKAJ JAIN

Worldwide Published by

Pendown Press

**PENDOWN PRESS**

An ISO 9001 & ISO 14001 Certified Co.,

**Regd. Office:** 2525/193, 1st Floor, Onkar Nagar-A,

Tri Nagar, Delhi-110035

**Ph.:** 09350849407, 09312235086

**E-mail:** info@pendownpress.com

**Branch Office:** 1A/2A, 20, Hari Sadan, Ansari Road,

Daryaganj, New Delhi-110002

**Ph.:** 011-45794768

**Website:** PendownPress.com

**First Edition:** 2023

**ISBN:** 978-93-5554-596-1



*Layout and Cover Designed by* Pendown Graphics Team

*Printed and Bound in India by* Thomson Press India Ltd.

*Dedicated to my Isht, The Ultimate
Guru, Gurus, Coaches, Parents, Family,
Friends and Entrepreneurs.*

# Contents

# Preface

*"When India speaks of becoming self-reliant, it doesn't advocate a self-centred system. In India's self-reliance; there is a concern for the whole World's happiness, cooperation and peace."*

~Hon'ble PM Shri Narendra Modi

An **Aatma Nirbhar Bharat** is well set to take back its ancient status and glory in the arena of International Trade once again. As global order gets reset, the ancient 'Trusted Relationship' based Business models of Indian Merchants who played a prominent role in global trade become highly relevant for Entrepreneurs of **Micro, Small and Medium Enterprises (MSMEs).** Indian MSME Entrepreneurs can easily leverage these principles to transform into Global MNCs in the post-Covid Global Order.

In my **Vanijya Sadhna** for over the last 31 years, I have gained the reputation as the Global MNC Coach following these eternal principles. And that is exactly what I am sharing in this book.

MSME is an inclusive term that encompasses a broad spectrum of businesses. Even mobile cart vendors, small shopkeepers and housewives running small home-based enterprises fall in the purview of MSMEs.

With all my experience, I can safely say that every MSME owner aspires to or dreams of transitioning into a Multinational Corporation (MNC) at some point in their entrepreneurial journey.

While many people may see this as mere wishful thinking, I can assure you that with the right guidance and following the right path, every MSME has the potential to become an MNC. However, the time taken to make this transition may be different for every Enterprise, depending on their typical situation.

With the abundance of opportunities available in the present world scenario, it is the best time for MSME owners to take the leap of faith powered by targeted guidance to scale up their business and make themselves **Aatma Nirbhar** (Self-Reliant) while spreading their empire globally.

So, stay with me through the following pages and stay excited as I share with you the secrets to navigating the challenges of transitioning from an MSME to an MNC smoothly, safely and speedily.

**~Jai Jinendra**
*CMA. Pankaj Jain*

NOTES:

# Why This Book?


**~C.K Prahlad's line that inspired Ratan Tata**

As I shared earlier, this is the best time to manifest the dream that every MSME owner holds in their heart to scale up their business to the highest level and take it global.

This brings us to the next logical question: **What is it about MNCs that every business owner aspires to be one?**

The reasons everyone aspires to be an MNC are because:

- An MNC has a global presence and, hence, a broader market penetration.

- It operates at a much larger scale of business.

- Due to its worldwide presence and bigger markets, an MNC has higher profit earnings.

- An MNC has a high potential for growth due to its larger scale of operations and a wider playing field.

- An MNC has a unique and recognizable Brand Identity & Value.

However, transitioning to an MNC from an MSME is not easy. The challenges are many. And that is where this book comes in.

- In this book, we will first learn what an MNC is and what its advantages are.

- Then, keeping the world business scenario in perspective, we will thoroughly understand the Indian context of global business.

- Next, we will identify and understand the 4 types of enterprises.

- Having understood all the above, we will embark on understanding the new Global Business Model post the Covid-19 Pandemic and its lingering impact.

- Finally, I will share with you the critical steps to successfully transition & transform your Enterprise from an MSME to an MNC.

In keeping with the endeavour of being self-reliant, I am on a mission to guide 10,000 MSMEs and launch them firmly onto the trajectory of global dominance by becoming an MNC. This book is a part of my service journey to fulfil this mission.

## NOTES:

# Who Am I?

*"Finance is all about business,*
*and business is all about people."*

~CMA. Pankaj Jain

Above is the Key Learning from my 27 years of experience working at senior level Finance and Business leadership roles…

Ok, so having read so far, I am sure there is another question crowding your mind. **"Who is Pankaj Jain, and why should I listen to him?"**

So as you know by now, My name is Pankaj Jain.

An alumnus of IIM Calcutta, I am a CMA, CS, AMT, and a Certified  Corporate Director. **I am also the creator of the Msme2MNC Model.**

Filled with the vibrant spirit of entrepreneurship fortified with over 31 years of diversified experience across a broad spectrum of industries, I have a proven track record of turning around the financial position of several companies through dynamic initiatives and helping them achieve exponential growth even in challenging times.

While working at top-level corporate positions as a VP, CFO, CEO, & Director, I have successfully led the growth of reputed business houses such as Super Seals, IAP, ERA Infra, and the Logix Group to the next level against all odds.

I have managed numerous strategic business initiatives involving Venture Formation, Business Modelling, Strategic Financial Planning, Corporate Alliances, Demergers, Divestments, Cost Optimization, Business Restructuring, Capital Structuring, Corporate Governance and Corporate Financing for successful businesses with global footprints.

I have also successfully raised funds for projects (including mega infrastructure projects under Public Private Partnership) with a cost of over Rs. 15000 crores from domestic and foreign sources.

Additionally, I am associated with many socio-economic initiatives in various capacities, including Founder President/ Chairman of the Indian Society of Management Accountants, Infra and Real Estate Foundation, Young Entrepreneurs Network, Indian RERA Forum, Bhartiya Global MSME Forum and have the privilege of being a mentor to many startups to help them achieve sustainability and scalability in their businesses.

I live, work and inspire others with this simple philosophy **"Those who Dream the Most, Try the Most, Do the Most..."**

My driving force is the belief that **"If someone can do it, we can also do it and even better."**

And my magic mantra for winning at business is to **Collaborate, Collaborate & Collaborate,** which I firmly believe in. We do not grow in isolation; we are stronger when we pool our resources and combine our strengths and core capabilities.

I am honoured to share with you some of my accolades…

Recipient of GOLD Medal for Best Performance.

Regular Jury member of Asia One, a Dubai-based leading Global media group which evaluates Rating for the Top 100 Brands of India, Asia and the World.

Mentor to many Startups, Entrepreneurs and MSMEs with the objective of helping them to achieve SUSTAINABILITY, SCALABILITY and SUCCESS of their Businesses in the Global Arena.

Guest faculty to leading Business Schools, Professional Institutes and Business Forums.

## Advisor on Boards of various Institutions

**Also, let me share with you my Investment Outlook in brief:**

Collaborating with entrepreneurs to achieve SUSTAINABILITY, scalability and Success of their businesses with GLOBAL Footprints…

**Mission:** Build self-sustainable institutions responsible for sustainable INCLUSIVE growth of the UNIVERSE…

**Philosophy:** Do not invest in the business. Invest in PEOPLE running the business…

**Interest Areas:** Tech-based solutions for Environment, MSME sector, Infra and Real Estate.

**My Sutra:** Connect, Collaborate and Co-create

You can always stay in touch with me @

- pjainonline@gmail.com
- +91 9312213765
- www.CmaPankajJain.in
- in.linkedin.com/in/cmapankajjain
- youtube.com/channel/UCZBtd6l17_5uIa1nyIiekSA
- twitter.com/cmapankajjain
- www.instagram.com/cmapankajjain/
- facebook.com/public/cmapankajjain
- www.slideshare.net/search?q=pjainonline

NOTES: ✎

---

# Is This Book For Me ?

*"Navigating your business to the next level is not merely a choice; it is your responsibility."*

~CMA. Pankaj Jain

In our series of questions, let's address the third critical question in your mind right now. I am certain you are wondering, "Is this book for me?"

Yes, this book is an absolute must-read for you if you are:

- An aspiring entrepreneur.
- An Entrepreneur, including a Startup owner.
- A Business Owner.
- A Professional of any kind.
- A Bureaucrat.
- A Politician.
- An Academician.
- A Student.
- Or even an MNC looking for the next level of growth.

The world post-pandemic is poised at a critical juncture. New ways of interacting and doing business have evolved, and only those who adapt and keep pace with the fast-changing global scenario will be able to survive and thrive.

If you have a vision for being self-reliant and running a successful and profitable global enterprise. **It is time to act Now!** And you are holding the Key to that doorway to success in your hands. So let's dive deep into it…

From my extensive experience and deep research into the challenges and concerns of MSMEs I understand that while things may differ a bit from sector to sector but nearly all of them have a similar set of challenges that they are SEEKING Solutions for…

- ✓ You inevitably face bottlenecks in your business and want to have a sound system in place to Bounce back higher and faster.
- ✓ You want to beat the competition and Stay ahead of the crowd.
- ✓ You want to make your business a Brand to reckon with.
- ✓ You want to have a Dashboard of your business at your Fingertips.
- ✓ You want to establish a Model for achieving Sustainable Inclusive Growth for your National Economy.
- ✓ You want to Run your Business without you.
- ✓ You want to Make Money even when you Sleep.
- ✓ You want more Quality Time for you and your Family.
- ✓ You want more Happiness in your Life.

If you answered YES to any, many or all of these, then this book is definitely for you!

## NOTES:

# The Core Areas of Transformation

*"Our Greatest Glory is not in never Falling,*
*but in Rising Everytime We Fall."*

**~Acharya Vasunandi Ji Muniraj**

Your journey of transforming your MSME into an MNC will involve transformation at the deepest level in 3 core areas.

1. Personal Transformation

2. Enterprise Transformation

3. Business Transformation

One level of transformation is your Personal Transformation.

# Personal Transformation

Your personal transformation begins with understanding and discovering yourself.

1. **Knowing Yourself**

    **a.** The first step is understanding who you are because YOU are the most important person in your Life. Everything, every relationship, and every circumstance exist because of you. Of course, there are external factors that impact your Life, but everything is driven by you. How you respond to these external factors is what creates your Life.

    **b.** The most important question to understand is, why are you here? Each of us is a unique being with our own set of skills, interests and impact. What one person brings to the table, the other perhaps cannot. So understand that no matter your age, gender, status, education etc., each of us serves a purpose on this planet, so never doubt your worth.

    **c.** What is your purpose? Once you understand that you have a purpose to fulfil, the next logical step is to identify what that purpose is. True success will find you once you follow and live your purpose.

**d.** Life is such that it never moves in a straight line; therefore, it is guaranteed that at some time or the other, you might get thrown off track. At such times you must have something that reminds you to get back on track. So it is important to identify what brings you back to your purpose.

## 2. Balancing your Soul, Mind and Body

For sustainable success, it is important that all your actions must be aligned with your purpose. This basically means that your desire, thoughts and actions must be one. Only then will there exist a balance of your Soul, Mind & Body. To give your best, it is important that you must be healthy spiritually, mentally and physically.

## 3. Make it a Core Purpose of your Life to Serve Others

Success and prosperity come to us and stay with us only when our intent and purpose move from being merely self-centred to being selfless. To grow big, we must think big. We must have the intent to serve others while creating abundance for ourselves.

Before you embark on your business transformation, it is necessary to work on yourself, and the best way to work on yourself is-

---

**Focus on yourself—**
**You are the Result of your own THOUGHTS,**
**WORDS & ACTIONS!**

---

This is your one and only path to Miracles that will lead you to Global Dominance…..

Nothing will ever change no matter how many homes, cities, businesses or employees you change; things will only change when your behaviour and actions change, and these will change only when your thoughts and words change.

I have a simple mantra for transformation that can truly give you global success-

# विश्व

**It means the WORLD**

**And if you look at it closely and understand deeper,**

**what is the World made up of-**

**विश्व = वि + श + व्**

**वि = विचार (Thoughts), श= शब्द (Words),**

**व्= व्यवहार (Actions)**

To transform your business, you must first transform yourself, and two things are key to transforming yourself:

1. **You must always have an open mind and an attitude toward learning.** When you have an open mind, you believe anything is possible, and from this belief comes all creation and success. If you are not open to possibilities, you are limiting yourself, and a limited mindset is like a cage you make for yourself. You must greet every person and circumstance as a learning opportunity; even failure can teach you lessons on what needs to be avoided and what more needs to be done. We will talk about this more in the next point.

2. **You must not fear failure and not let it stop you from taking action.** So many people I meet are hesitant to think and act big because they are afraid of failing. Here I have a radical piece of advice for you. Do not be scared of failure, do not shy away from it. Instead, embrace your failure. For who fails? Only those who try, and there is no way of winning and succeeding without trying!

**Therefore failure is something that no one can avoid. It is inevitable and is a part of every successful journey.**

Let me share with you a secret about dealing with failure. **Often uninvited guests will drop in at your house, you do not like it, but do you stop living in your home from the fear of these guests?** Do not run away from failure. Think of it like an uninvited guest; when that guest arrives on your doorstep, do you run out of your backdoor or hide in your room... No?

Instead, you open the door, put on your best smile (even if it is fake) and greet them, ask them to come in, offer them tea/coffee and all courtesy but make sure they do not let them stay for too long. Soon you see them off at the door.

That is exactly what you do with failure, and neither do you run away from it. Nor do you let it stay and impact you for long. Some entrepreneurs I have seen let failure scar them for a long time; they stay rooted in fear and do not move forward. Failure is unavoidable, but it is not permanent. You learn from it and move on.

Therefore, let go of the fear of failure because when you let go of fear, you give your best and operate from a place of passion.

Now that you understand the importance and the basics of **Personal Transformation,** continue to work on yourself through the right routine of yoga, meditation, visualization, affirmations and reading the teachings of great masters and Gurus, as learning and growing are ongoing processes.

The second level of transformation is your Enterprise Transformation.

# Enterprise Transformation

**What is even more important than business transactions is the vehicle of your business journey- your Enterprise.**

*Enterprises are the growth engines of businesses and the economy.*

Therefore your business growth depends on the kind of Enterprise you choose to run. From my entire experience and research, I have surmised that there are four types of enterprises.

**A Person Driven Enterprise** is an enterprise that is dependent on its owner, and all decisions are taken by the owner. If you choose this type of Enterprise as your business vehicle, then it is like riding a **Motorcycle;** while you may be able to manoeuvre your way in & out of challenges, you will not be able to face weather changes, and also you will be able to grow only to a limited level as your vehicle can only handle so much.

**A People Driven Enterprise** is one where there is an owner and a team of professionals guiding it. This kind of business vehicle can be said to be an upgrade to a **Car.** You can travel faster & safer, and there is more scope for growth compared to a person-driven Enterprise.

**A Process Driven Enterprise** is one where along with the owner and the team of professionals, there are standard processes also in place to handle all necessary activities and operations. Using this business vehicle is like having a **Train** at your disposal. You can grow quite far and fast, and there is a lot of potential to grow.

**A Purpose Driven Enterprise** has everything that all the above three have, but here the purpose is the boss, you, your people and your processes are driven by the passion of that purpose. It is like flying an **Airplane,** and this is the most powerful growth engine. There is no limit to your potential, the World is your sky, and you can reach your destination superfast.

Therefore if you have to grow and make your mark as a successful India-based MNC like Tata, Mahindra, Birla, Infosys, Bharti, HDFC, ITC etc., it is imperative that you identify your purpose of doing business and then ensure that every word, thought and action is aligned toward that purpose.

*Let's Build PURPOSEFUL Enterprises*
*which can be GLOBALLY Sustainable,*
*Scalable and Super Successful.*

## NOTES:

# A Purpose-Driven MNC

*"It's only when companies are clear about their purpose, have clearly communicated it, and it is understood by the team that companies can achieve both unity of effort and distributed decision making."*

**~Marc Koehler**

Now that we have been talking for quite some time about transforming your business into an MNC, it's important to understand what exactly an MNC is and why everyone aspires to be one.

"A multinational corporation (MNC) is a company that has business offices and operations in at least one country (or more) other than its home country. These operations are often managed from a central office headquartered in the home country."

Here I want you to clearly understand that an enterprise that is merely exporting goods to another country or even many countries does not qualify as an MNC.

Now the question arises, why does every business owner wish to transform their business into an MNC?

The answer is simple but manifold:

- An MNC has a **Large Scale of Business Operations.**
- Due to its large scale of business, an MNC has **Higher Profit Earnings.**
- It has a **Wide Global Presence.**
- Since it has a global presence, it offers a **Higher Potential for Growth.**
- An MNC also has a **Popular Brand Value & Recognition.**

Here I'll let you in on a secret—there is something even better than being an MNC. **It's a Global MNC.**

An MNC is one that simply replicates the business model it uses in its own country in all the other countries of its operations, whereas a Global MNC is one that tweaks its business model to suit the needs and sensibilities of its local area of operations. **Such enterprises think global but act local.** This helps the local people identify with these companies, leading to their success.

## Purpose is the Fuel that Drives the Wagon of Success

However, even beyond a Global MNC exists a type of Enterprise that succeeds and becomes a brand beyond all benchmarks of success!

This Enterprise is a **Purpose Driven MNC.** A purpose-driven MNC is one that does not merely focus on generating business and financial success; rather, it has as its core value and mission something beyond numbers. It has the intent and desire to serve people and contribute to society.

One of the greatest examples of a purpose-driven MNC exists in our own country itself. It is none other than the Tata Group.

The founder of this group, Jamshed ji Tata, stated in writing that their purpose of doing business was to contribute to the economic growth of India and to give back to the people. And that is what has been driving them till today.

They are a group worth billions of dollars, but that is just one of their success criteria; they are known and recognized for reasons beyond that.

NOTES:

# Reviving India's Ancient Glory of Global Trade With The New Business Model

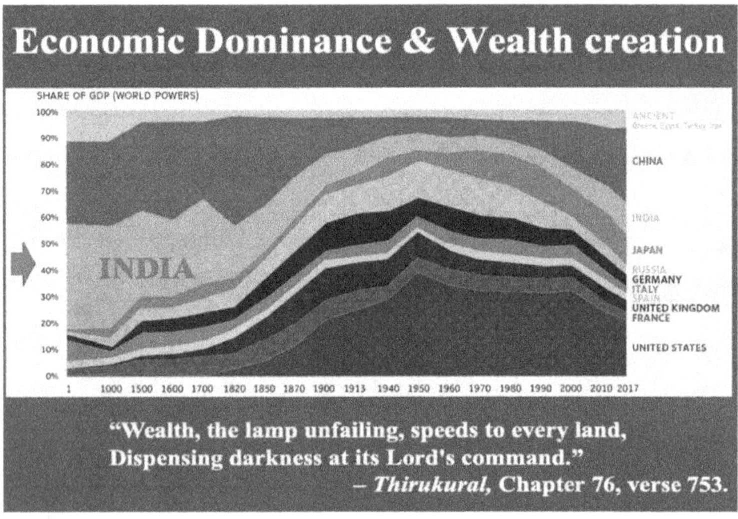



At one point in time, Ancient India had nearly 40% share in Global Trade.

> *"Take care of the earth,*
> *and she will take care of you."*
>
> **~Traditional Proverb**

If you wish to embark on your journey of transforming your MSME into an MNC, the time is now.

Post-pandemic, the field of opportunities is wide open and inviting. The World has shrunk due to technology, and India has moved up in the rankings of countries and their ease of doing business.

You can join the revolutionary list of businesses that are striving to revive India's traditional trade glory and dominance. Just to give you a little context, if we were to look at the trade history of various prominent countries such as the USA, China, Italy, France, Germany, the UK and India for the last 1000 years, we would find some unexpected things.

Look carefully at the picture below, which depicts the timeline on one axis and the trade share on the other.

You will find that at one period of time, India held the lion's share and dominated the world trade. Also, you will notice that India has been a consistent player throughout, with a significant contribution. With the current business scenario in our country and the World, **it is the right time to begin transforming your MSME into an MNC and contribute to India's economy and restore its Business Glory.**

## The New-Age Business Model

However, we operate in a new age today, and the new-age dynamics of business have changed radically. Today the World is poised on the verge of an ecological challenge where we might lose the planet we live on. Climate change, environmental pollution and other hazards are real threats.

The pandemic has taught us that anything catastrophic can happen and upset our cart at any time. We have all been through the challenging times of the pandemic, so I really don't need to elaborate on it any further.

***So here's a simple deduction- if there is no environment, obviously, there will be no enterprises.***

We are all aware of the time-tested QCDS Model of doing business, which emphasizes Quality, Cost, Delivery& Service.

However, with the changing times, another criterion has been added to the mix.

This new criterion is the ENVIRONMENT.

| Traditional QCDS Business Model |
|---|
| Quality >>>>>>>>>>>>> Up |
| Cost <<<<<<<<<<<<<< Down |
| Delivery = = = = == = = = On Time |
| Service =  =  =  =  =   = = On Demand |

**Henceforth only those enterprises will succeed and survive who care for the environment's welfare and will operate in an eco-friendly, sustainable manner, no matter the industry.**

| New-Age EQCDS Business Model |
| --- |
| Environment = = = = = Protected |
| => No. 1 Priority for Every Business |
| Quality >>>>>>>>>>>> Up |
| Cost <<<<<<<<<<<<<< Down |
| Delivery = = = = = = = = = On Time |
| Service = = = = = = = == = On Demand |

**If protecting the environment in all possible ways that your business permits is not your priority, it will indeed be difficult for your business to survive, leave alone thrive {It can even be things as small as not printing anything unless necessary, using zero plastic, having an eco-friendly building, rain-water-harvesting etc.} everything has an impact.**

And as you continue to transform at a personal level and enterprise level, you must simultaneously work on transforming your MSME into an MNC through the Business Transformation Practices listed below, which I will share with you in detail in the forthcoming chapters.

## NOTES:

# Business Transformation Practices

I am sharing below with you the important business transformation practices that are essential to evolving into an MNC from an MSME.

## Develop an MNC Mindset

Before you take any action to become an MNC, you have to first develop the mindset of becoming an MNC. For this, you must believe that becoming an MNC is possible. When you perform from the place of possibilities, your vision is expanded. It also means being open to learning and adopting new practices and technology always.

## Focus on Value Creation

Value creation is one of the core mantras of success. It is the foundational bedrock of business. It's what sets you apart from your competition, fosters customer loyalty and gives a distinct identity and branding to your Enterprise. It is the starting point of any and every business transformation.

## Start with the Mindset of Creating Value for Others

If you wish to become an MNC, you cannot afford to be just another commodity in the market; you have to go above and beyond the requirements of everyone in your chain of operations, Be it your customers, your employees, your vendors or your collaborators. All your stakeholders must receive beyond expectations. Successful businesses create value with each transaction. In order to create value it is essential that you:

- **Understand the Value Creation Chain and Activities** [The image below gives you an overview of the primary and secondary value chain activities.]

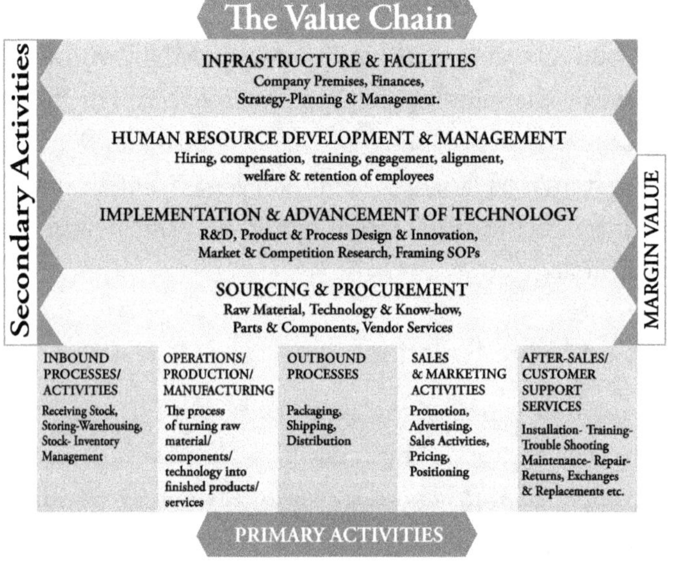


- **Value Stream Mapping**-In order to create value of the highest possible standard, you should implement the process of value stream mapping through which you must visualize, analyze and then list out improvements to all the steps involved in that particular process of your value chain.

- **Create a System to Measure Value Creation**-Once you have understood the activities of the value chain and put in place practices to add value to each transaction, it is important to monitor and review your value creation activities. For this, you must have a system to measure your activities and tweak them to bring them on track when needed.

- **Global Value Chain (Supply Chain)**- In order to transition from an MSME to an MNC, it is important to focus on building a global supply chain, either physically or online, depending on your mode of business/type of product or service.

## Follow The Triple WIN Formula

A great thumb rule to always ensure success with service is the Triple WIN Formula. Simply put, this formula means that for every transaction or decision you make, you should stop and think of how it impacts not just the two parties directly involved in the transaction but also the other parties (third parties) that it may impact.

This formula takes care of the interest of third parties who are not a direct part of transactions between two main parties.

## Building Trust-Based Relationships Globally

Being ethical and authentic in all your transactions and delivering value through your products/services will earn you trust among customers and collaborators. Trust is the trigger that makes you the first choice to do business with.

## Back to Basics

This simple rule is another transformational mantra that all successful people and organizations use. No matter how complicated or entangled the issue may be, stripping it down to the basics always deescalates the situation.

So, whenever you face complex situations, instead of applying complex rules, resolve them by following simple ground rules which are very easy to understand.

## Be the Best Benchmark

In a world filled with 6 billion people, no one has the exact same face or the same fingerprints as you. You are Unique! What you can do, no one else can do. You are here for a purpose. So work on yourself and be the best version of yourself. Be your own highest benchmark. Do not compare yourself to anyone. Affirm "I do not compare or compete with others. I do not want to compare or compete with myself. I want to compare and compete with what I am today."

Do everything in your power to improve yourself continuously. Work toward your desires and wants. Dream big but keep your goals realistic because each time you achieve a goal, you will be motivated to reach even higher for the next goal.

## Benchmark with the Best

It is often said that you become the company you keep and ensure that the company you keep challenges you to be better and better each day. If you have to look up to or aspire toward anyone, make sure you keep the bar high and benchmark only with the best.

## Collaborate to Co-create (Global Collaboration)

As the saying goes, together, we are stronger. Collaborations are the Key to scaling up and transitioning to an MNC. With collaborations, you can get many advantages that would be challenging to have on your own.

- **Capabilities-** Through collaboration, you can gain new capabilities in areas where you might not be that strong.

- **Capital-** Having a collaborator can work 2 ways in terms of capital advantage; it can either help you reduce your capital investment burden, or it can help give you access to additional capital resources to scale up your operations.

- **Competition-** Collaborating with others in your field can help mitigate competition and be stronger together.

- **Customers-** Collaborating has another great advantage that can help you scale your business as it gives you access to your collaborator's customer base too.

- **Core Competency-** Collaborating with another enterprise can also give you a core competency that you were missing or add to your existing expertise. Either way, it's a win-win.

## Empower People

As I've already shared earlier, people are the core of business success. If you wish to establish yourself as a global enterprise, you must empower the people in your organization. Delegation and decentralization with accountability checks are the hallmarks of an MNC.

## Cost Intelligence

In today's global business scenario, China is the leading player. They have dumped their low-cost products throughout the World and are purposely destroying the market with this strategy.

If Indian SMEs wish to dominate the world market, they need to be cost-smart and beat the competition with cost intelligence.

**Cost Intelligence is a most powerful tool** in your journey to transforming into an MNC.

**However, the entire definition of Cost and profit has changed today.**

Today, the Cost is not what we are incurring.

Earlier, the sale/selling price was determined by the cost price and the profit desired, i.e.,

$$\textbf{Sale Price = Cost + Profit}$$

However, today it is not that simple. Today you have to operate from a cost-based approach.

Today you cannot randomly add any desired profit margin to your cost price and sell.

Today your sale price is determined by what the customers are willing to pay, and the competitors allow...

**Now transformed into**

**Cost-Based Approach, i.e. Cost = Market Determined Sale Price - Target Profit**

Therefore the essential thing here is to

*"Optimize Cost to increase profit."*

## Cash Flow Dynamics

Most people make the mistake of believing that cash flow and Profitability are the same. To transition successfully into an MNC, you must understand that they are not interchangeable.

Cash flow represents the cash coming into (inflows) and going out of (outflows) from the business. Cash inflows and outflows **show liquidity, meaning how much cash you have on hand**. Liquidity is a short-term measurement seen through a cash flow statement that tells you whether you can reduce immediate financial liabilities.

**Whereas Profitability** is a long-term measurement of success. It represents the income and expenses of the business. When expenses are subtracted from income, the result is profit or (loss).

**Measuring & monitoring your cash flow is essential** to remain financially healthy and being prepared to meet your financial commitments and other needs for scaling up your business.

Also, you must understand the working capital cycle, as it is an important financial concept for any business. It helps you understand how long your Money will be tied up in stock and inventory. Together with your cash flow statement, the working capital cycle can be used to predict and manage how Money flows in and out of your business, as well as ensure you have enough cash on hand to meet your commitments.

Additionally, you must perform a critical analysis of your **CAPEX** (Capital Expenditure, meaning major long-term expenses such as buildings, properties, machinery, vehicles etc.) and **OPEX** (Day-to-day expenses such as salaries, rent, utilities such as electricity etc. and taxes) to determine where you can modify and optimize your Cost and investment strategy and whether the returns are commensurate or not.

A dynamic projected cash flow is an absolute must-have in today's fast-changing scenario. If the pandemic has taught us one thing, it is to be prepared for the worst-case scenario.

The capability of an organization to navigate through significant instability determines its long-term financial health. A cash-flow forecast model serves as an early warning sign of a company's future business health by preparing for a variety of future circumstances.

Having a model that is dynamic, easily updated for changing conditions, and able to step in as a fire extinguisher in a furnace room is a necessity and not a luxury.

## Knowledge Organization

From all my experience, I have come to the understanding that while Indian MSMEs have a lot of knowledge, they are not adept at knowledge management and organization. This one trait is absolutely necessary to transform into an MNC.

After many hits and trials, through many learnings and challenges, Indian MSMEs discover great ways and practices of doing things, yet they often fail to document these into SOPs (Standard Operation Procedures) to ensure smooth and consistent operations for better and standard results. Therefore one of the critical business transformations is to **Document what you practice**. US companies are very strong at this; this eliminates any personal biases and fluctuations.

And then there is the other side of this, which is **practising what you document**. Japanese enterprises are extremely strong at this. **If you want to go global, you must have in place procedures, guidelines and SOPs, and you must ensure that you follow those diligently.**

In today's times, if you do not leverage technology, you are sure to be left behind. Therefore if you are aiming for the big leagues, **it is essential to digitize your operations to the maximum possible limit.**

This digitization and standardization of operations will also **enable you to have remote access and control of your business,** which is essential to going global.

## Research and Development (R&D)

R&D is a valuable tool for ongoing development and continuous growth. R&D involves researching your market and your customer needs and developing new and improved products and services to fit these needs. Without investing in dedicated R&D, your business will stagnate. R&D is the means to innovation, and **innovation** will form the **core of differentiation and branding.** Companies that keep an attitude of continuous exploration to adopt new technology and techniques have a greater chance of success than businesses that don't. This can boost your business's competitive advantage in a crowded market.

# NOTES:

# Connect, Converse
# and Co-create with the Universe

In the pages above, I have shared with you the gateway to the portal of progress and transformation. Following and implementing these super tips and life-altering practices will set you firmly on the path to manifesting your dream of turning your MSME into an MNC.

Before we move on to the next section of the book dedicated to **"Testimonies of Truth"** from people who have already experienced this magic and fulfilled their dream under my mentorship, I have one more gem of wisdom to share with you.

Remember that all worldly, material and financial transformation is possible only when you are spiritually anchored; when you know that you are here for a purpose, then all universal energy supports you unconditionally in fulfilling that purpose.

And believe me; this is no new-age mambo jumbo- science has proven what spirituality has always proclaimed; that everything is energy and the universe functions through the language of vibration.

Therefore spend some time in meditation and introspection every day to sit and **connect with the universe.**

In this deep state of connection, the intuitive guidance and advice you receive as thoughts are invaluable; This is how **the universe converses with you.**

Ensure that you act on this intuitive guidance you receive because when you take guided action, you attract what you desire. The universe then sends you abundant support in the form of opportunities, people and resources etc. **This is how you co-create success and abundance with the universe.**

So take a few deep breaths to centre yourself and begin practising and implementing all that I have shared in this book so that your success story can be a part of the next edition of this book in the *"Testimonies of Truth"* section...

# Testimonies of Truth

In this section, I am sharing with you a few of the innumerable real-life transformational experiences that my clients & I have created as a team.

These are shared with the sincere intention of inspiring you to take action toward your dream/goal of journeying from a Msme to an MNC.

> ### Unparalleled Expertise- Invaluable Guidance
>
> "I cannot say enough good things about the Global MNC Coach and his mentorship services.
>
> His guidance has been invaluable in helping me understand the financial aspects of running a business and creating a Purpose Driven Enterprise.
>
> He has a unique ability to break down complex financial concepts into understandable and actionable steps, which has helped me make better decisions for my business.
>
> The coach's commitment to helping his clients succeed is truly remarkable, and his expertise in financial management and strategy is unparalleled. If you're looking to grow your business and create a lasting impact.
>
> I highly recommend working with this coach."
>
> **~Arvind Singh**
> *Managing Director*
> *Krasa International Pvt. Ltd*

## Sky-High Commitment & Care For Clients

"I had the pleasure of working with the Global MNC Coach for over a year, and I can confidently say that my business wouldn't be where it is today without his guidance.

His focus on creating a Purpose Driven Enterprise has not only helped us increase our profits but has also given our company a deeper sense of meaning and impact.

He truly cares about his clients and their success, and I would highly recommend his mentorship services to anyone looking to take their business to the next level."

**~Ashish Kaushik**
*Entrepreneur*

## Increased Income & Impact Exponentially!

"I highly recommend the mentorship services of this Global MNC Coach for any business owner looking to not only increase profits but also create a purpose-driven enterprise.

With his expert guidance and support, I was able to develop a financial strategy that aligned with my business goals and values.

He provided me with invaluable insights into financial planning, budgeting, and forecasting and helped me identify areas for improvement in my business operations.

His approach is highly personalized and tailored to my specific needs, and he is always available to answer any questions and provide ongoing support.

Thanks to his mentorship, my business is not only more profitable, but it is also making a positive impact on the world. I cannot recommend their services enough!"

**~Rajesh Jain**
*Director Arihant Infrra Realtors Pvt. Ltd.*

Using the strategies shared in this book, your testimony could be a part of this section in the next edition of this book.

The time to take action toward your dream of building a purpose-driven global enterprise is NOW!

Reach out for a free one-to-one discovery session at

📞 9312213765

✉ pjainonline@gmail.com

# NOTES:

## NOTES:

9 789355 545961